CONTENTS

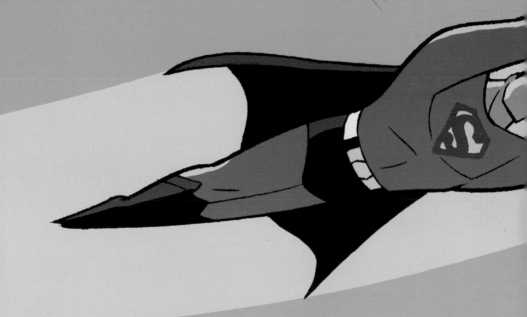

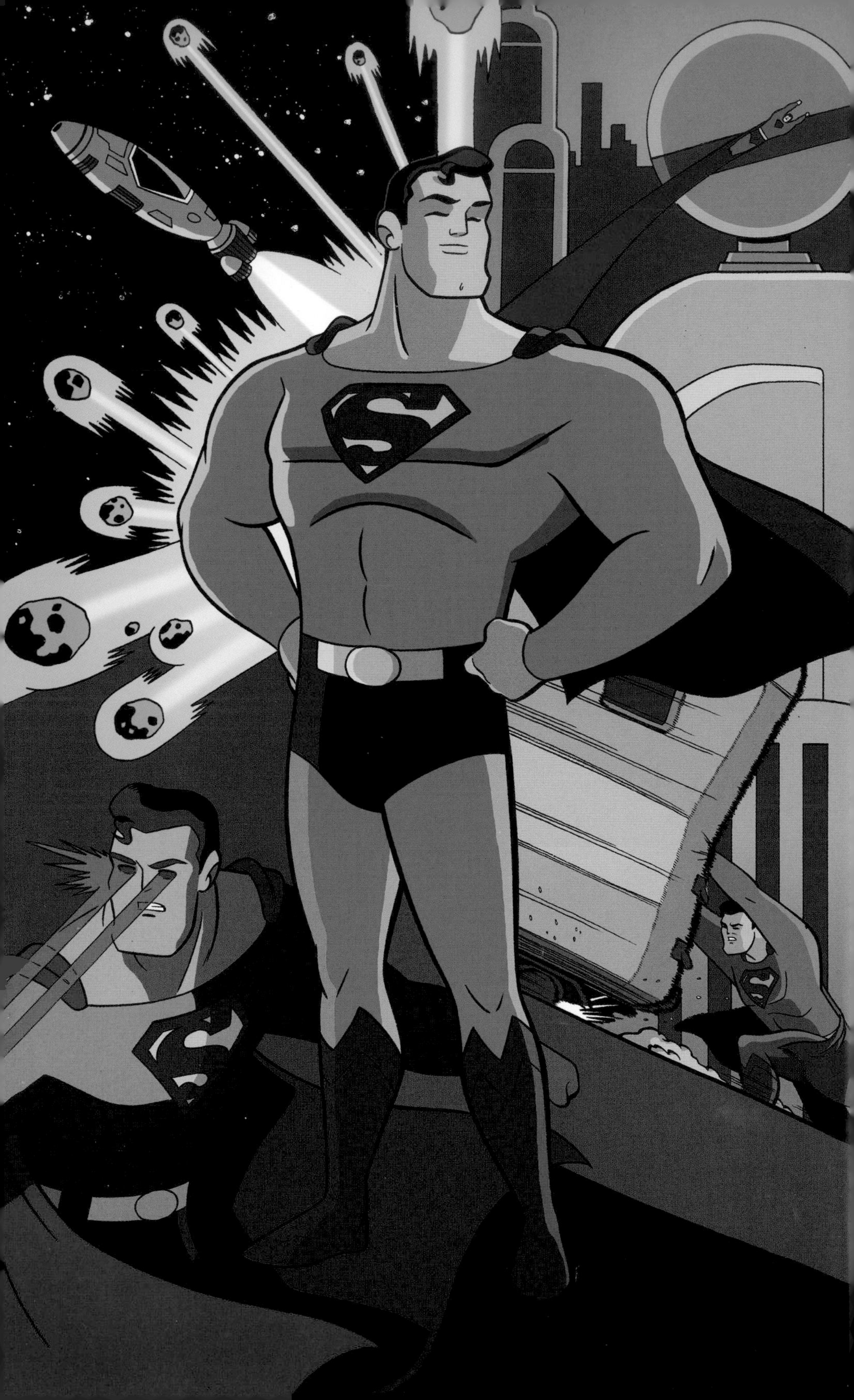

Born among the stars.
Raised on planet Earth.
With incredible powers,
he became the
World's Greatest Super Hero.
These are...

THE AMAZING ADVENTURES OF SUPERMAN!™

Chapter 1

A NEW ENEMY

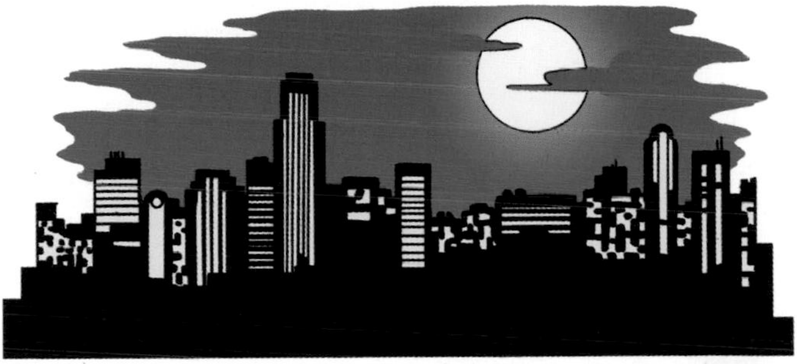

For once, the night is calm in Gotham City. High above Batman's home town, a blue and red object streaks through the sky.

It's ... Superman!

"What a great night,"
the hero says. "I love flying
through Gotham City on my
way home to Metropolis."

BOOM!!

An explosion from below

rattles Superman's ears!

"What was that?" he

asks. "I'd better find out."

Superman quickly lands

on the street. Someone is

destroying the city. It's none

other than ... Batman!

Chapter 2

AN OLD FRIEND

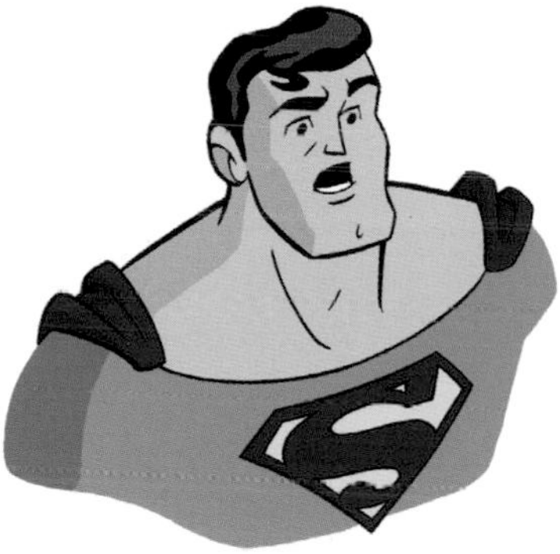

"What are you doing?"

Superman asks his friend.

"Having a little fun,"

Batman says, racing towards

Superman. He strikes the

Man of Steel with his fist!

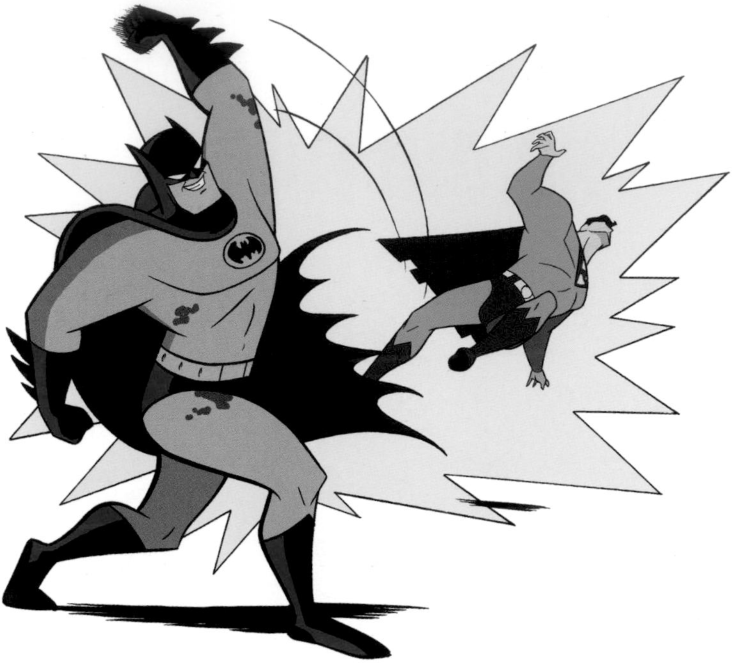

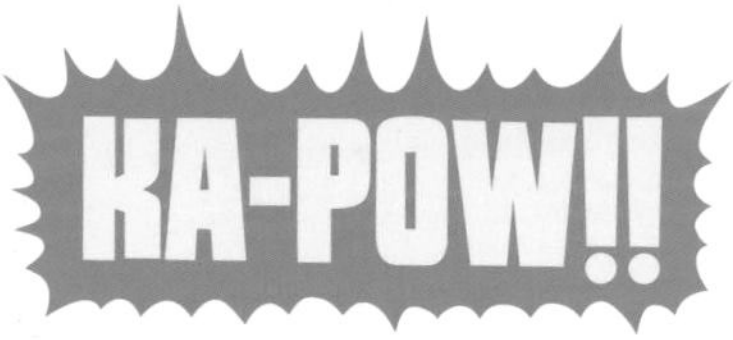
KA-POW!!

The mighty blow sends Superman across the street.

"Where did Batman get that strength?" the hero asks himself.

Superman doesn't have time to think. Batman charges him again.

WHOOSH! A red and yellow tornado suddenly appears. It twirls right into Batman!

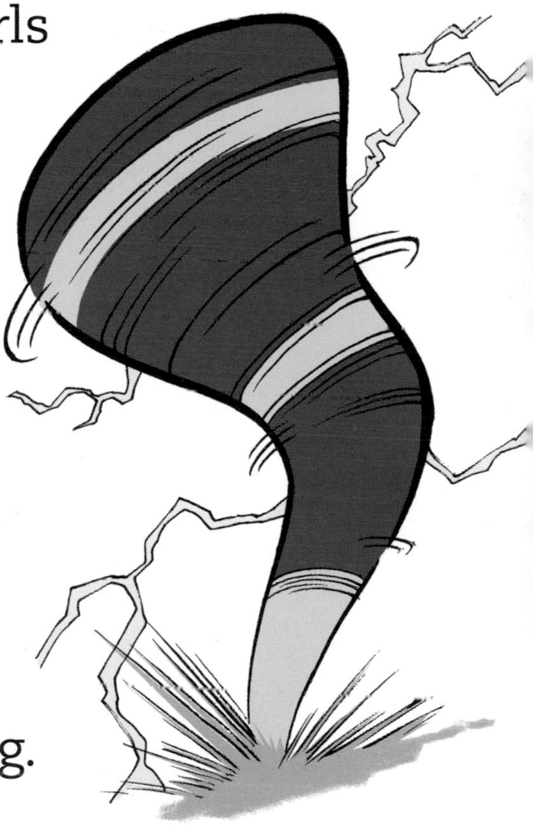

The gust sends Batman through a nearby building.

When the tornado stops,

the Fastest Man Alive

stands in its place.

"What's wrong with

Batman?" asks The Flash.

"I'm not sure," replies

Superman. "But he needs to

be stopped – and quick!"

"Quick shouldn't be a problem," The Flash says with a smile.

On the next street along, the heroes spot Batman inside the Batmobile.

"You're not getting away that easily," says The Flash.

Superman grabs Batman from the high-tech car. "Got you!" the hero says. "This battle ends here!"

"Battle? What battle?" Batman asks, puzzled. "I'm on the trail of Clayface."

"Clayface?" The Flash

asks. "The shape-shifting

super-villain?"

"The one and only," says

Batman. The hero points at

a muddy trail leading into

the sewer. "And he's slipped

away again."

Superman realizes he wasn't fighting Batman. He was fighting Clayface in disguise! "I'm sorry, Batman," he says.

"Save the apologies, guys," says Batman. He lifts a manhole cover from the street. "We've got a bigger mess to clean up."

Chapter 3

TIME FOR CHANGE

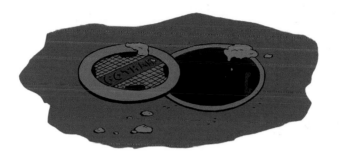

In the sewer, the three

heroes find Clayface. He is

still disguised as Batman.

"Stop right there!" they

shout at the sneaky villain.

Clayface spins.

"You three should still be
fighting each other!" shouts
the mudman.

"We've sorted out our
differences," says Batman.

"Yes," says Superman,
smiling. "People change."

"You can say that again!"

Clayface shouts. The villain

changes into a hulking,

mud-caked beast.

He attacks the heroes!

Batman flings a Batarang
at the villain. The metal
weapon sinks deep into
Clayface's gooey body.

"My weapons are
useless," says Batman.

"Stand back!" Superman shouts. The hero takes a deep breath. He lets out the chill of an arctic wind.

FWOOOOOOOOOOOSH!!

In an instant, Clayface freezes in his tracks!

Later, on the street

above, the heroes hand over

Clayface to the Gotham City

police. The villain is frozen

in a solid block of ice.

"He'll have plenty of time
to chill out," says Batman.

"Maybe he'll have time
to change, too," Superman
adds. "For the better."

"Well, I have to run," The
Flash says, dashing away.

"Until our next amazing adventure," Superman tells Batman.

The heroes shake hands tightly. They test each other's mighty strength.

"Don't push it, old pal," Batman says.

And so, a city – and a great friendship – has been saved!

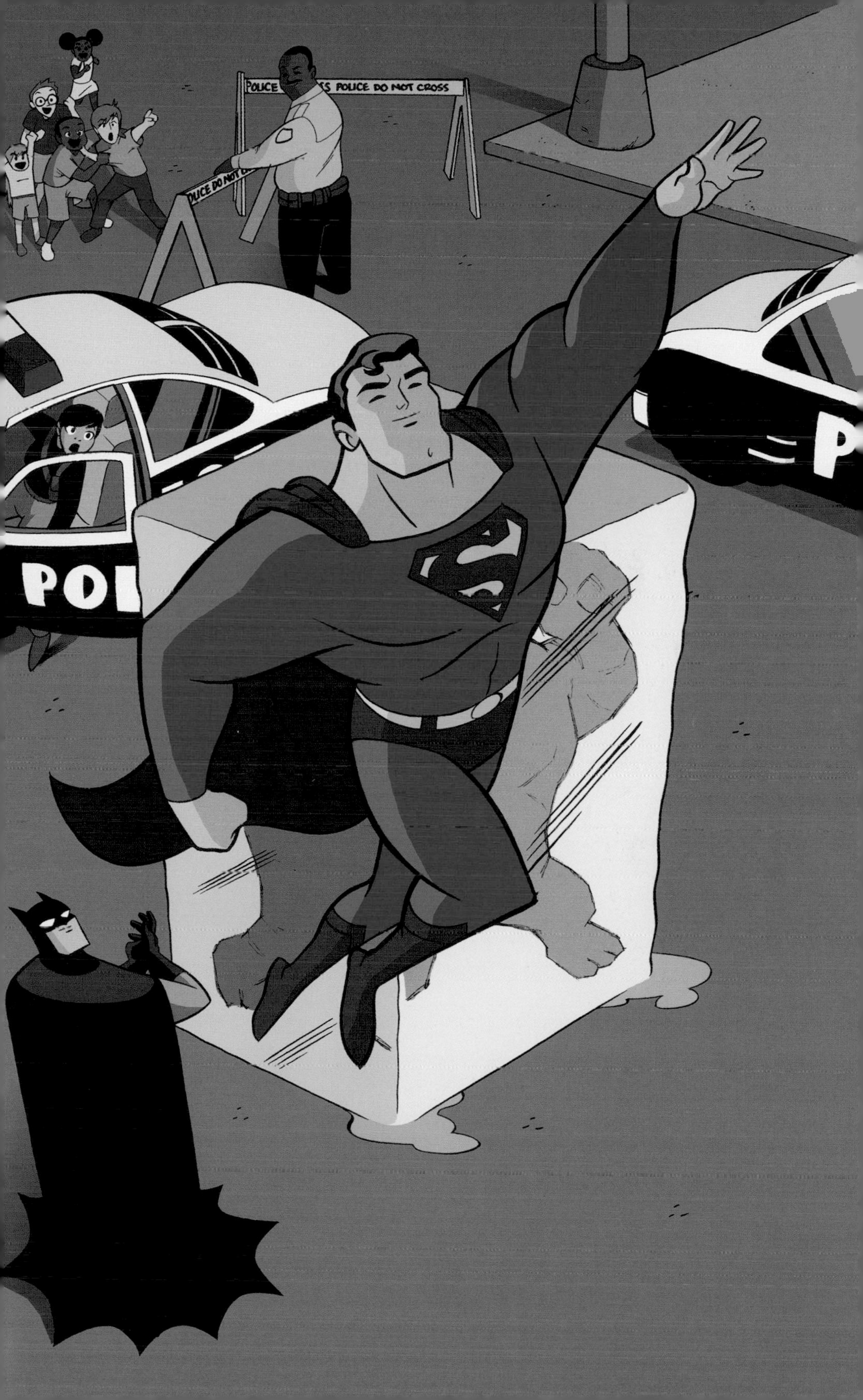

POLICE
POLICE DO NOT CROSS
POLICE DO NOT
POL
P

SUPERMAN'S SECRET MESSAGE!

Hey, kids! When a problem is too difficult for one person, what's the best way to solve it?

Use the code below to solve the secret message!

A	B	C	D	E	F	G	H	I	J	K	L	M

N	O	P	Q	R	S	T	U	V	W	X	Y	Z

apologies act of saying you're sorry for something

arctic very cold and wintry

Batarang metal, bat-shaped weapon used by Batman

disguise dressing in a way that hides who you really are

sewer underground pipe that carries away liquid and waste

super-villain very evil person

tornado whirling, funnel-shaped cloud that travels over land and usually causes damage

THE AMAZING ADVENTURES OF SUPERMAN!™

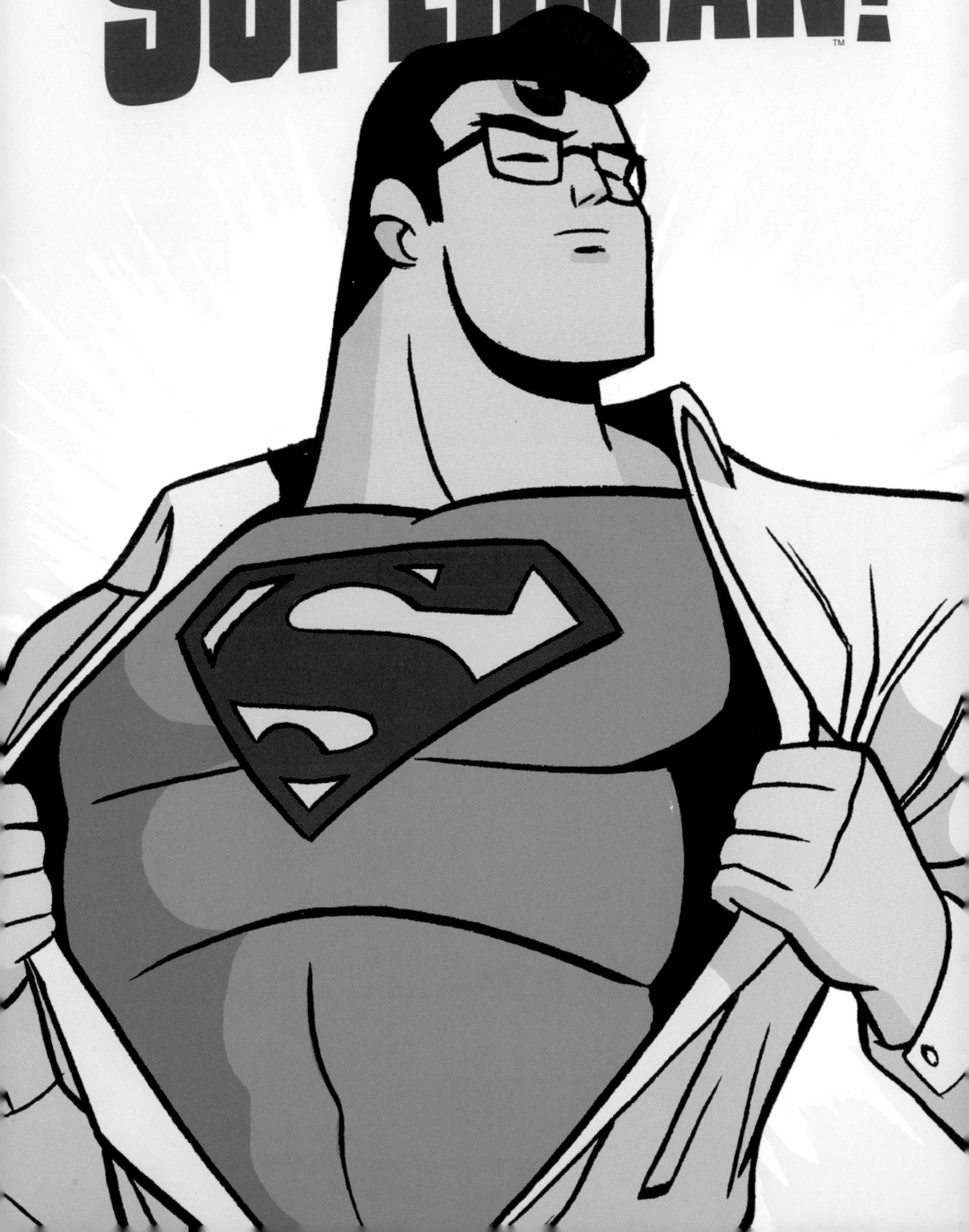

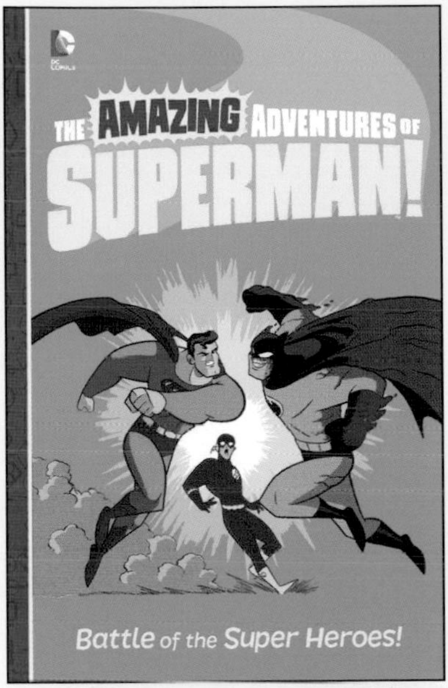
DC COMICS
THE AMAZING ADVENTURES OF
SUPERMAN!
Battle of the Super Heroes!

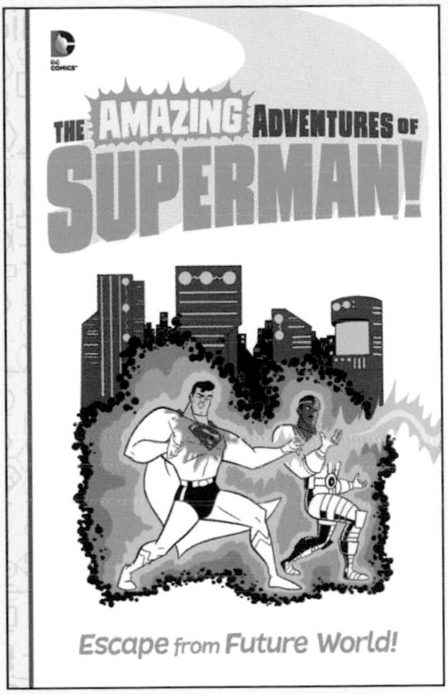
DC COMICS
THE AMAZING ADVENTURES OF
SUPERMAN!
Escape from Future World!

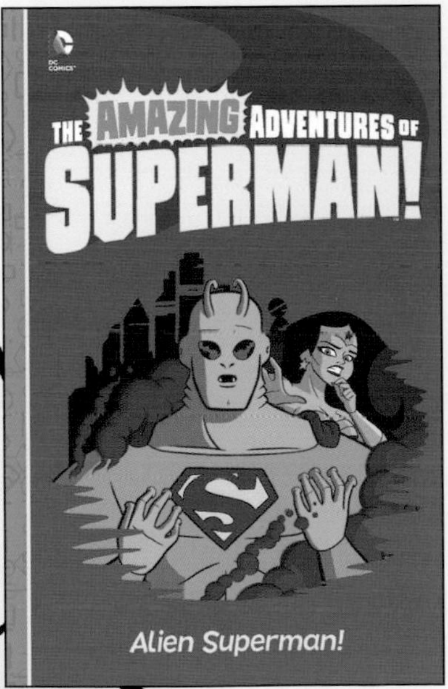
DC COMICS
THE AMAZING ADVENTURES OF
SUPERMAN!
Alien Superman!

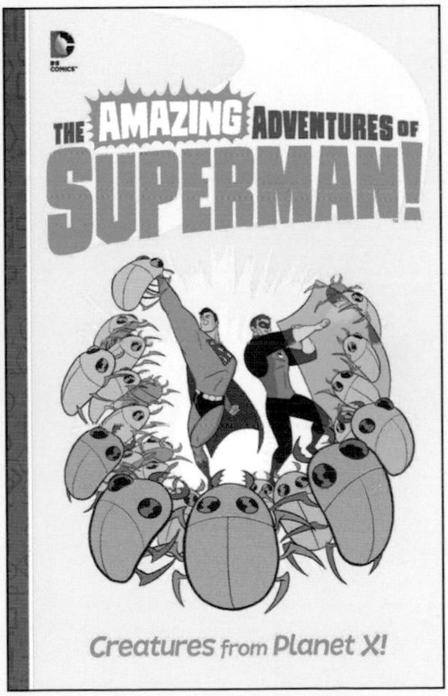
DC COMICS
THE AMAZING ADVENTURES OF
SUPERMAN!
Creatures from Planet X!

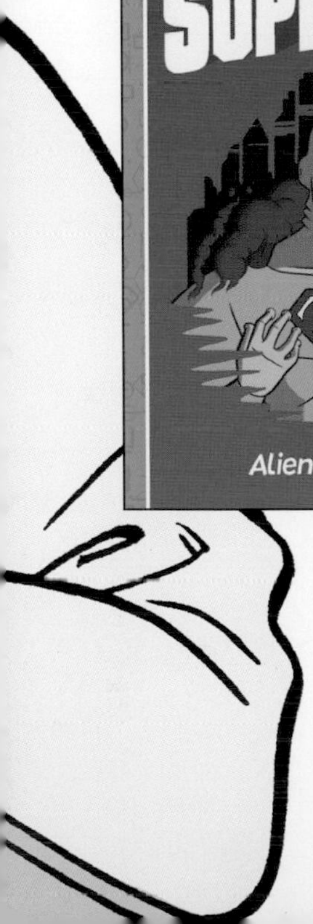

COLLECT THEM ALL!

only from . . . RAINTREE